WHIFF

or HOW THE BEAUTIFUL BIG FAT SMELLY BABY FOUND A FRIEND

For Emilio, with love
from Dad and Ian

A PICTURE CORGI BOOK : 0 552 546151

First published in Great Britain by Doubleday,
a division of Transworld Publishers

PRINTING HISTORY
Doubleday edition published 1999
Picture Corgi edition published 2000

5 7 9 10 8 6 4

Text copyright © Ian Whybrow 1999
Illustrations copyright © Russell Ayto 1999
Designed by Ian Butterworth

The right of Ian Whybrow to be identified as the author and
Russell Ayto as the illustrator of this work has been asserted in
accordance with the Copyright, Designs and Patents Act 1988

Picture Corgi Books are published by Transworld Publishers,
61-63 Uxbridge Road, London W5 5SA,
a division of The Random House Group Ltd,
in Australia by Random House Australia (Pty) Ltd,
20 Alfred Street, Milsons Point, Sydney, NSW 2061, Australia,
in New Zealand by Random House New Zealand Ltd,
18 Poland Road, Glenfield, Auckland 10, New Zealand
and in South Africa by Random House (Pty) Ltd,
Endulini, 5A Jubilee Road, Parktown 2193, South Africa

Printed in Singapore

WHIFF

or HOW THE BEAUTIFUL BIG FAT SMELLY BABY FOUND A FRIEND

Ian Whybrow
Illustrated by Russell Ayto

Picture Corgi Books

By a bend in the river lived
a beautiful big fat smelly baby warthog.

His mum and dad were very proud of him.
They called him Whiff.
They wanted him to make friends and be happy.

The Crocodiles lived on one side.
The Monkeys lived on the other side.
And right across the street lived the Littlebirds.

One day Mrs Crocodile knocked on the door.
She said:

My baby wants to play with your baby. But tell me, is your baby rough?

Oh no, my baby is NEVER rough.

So Whiff went next door and played very, very gently.

But then... down came some tickly quickly flies!
They tickled their ears and they tickled their eyes.

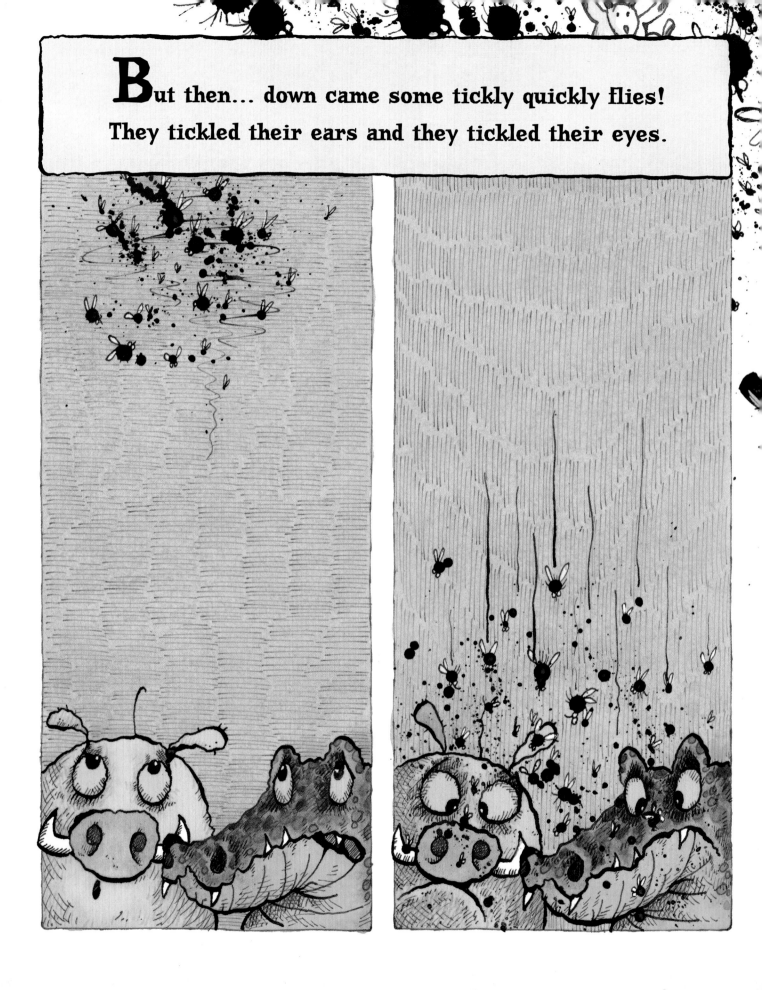

So the crocodile bit his teddy bears,
He bashed the table and he crashed the chairs,
His teeth went snap and his tail went wheee!
Down fell the pictures, one-two-three!

So Whiff the beautiful big fat smelly baby had to go home in disgrace.

So Whiff went next door to have tea with the Monkey babies.
He was on his best behaviour.

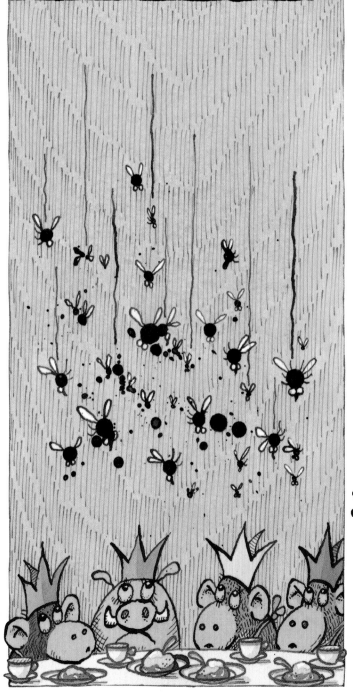

BUT... down came some tickly quickly flies! They tickled their ears and they tickled their eyes.

And cups and saucers flew through the air, And plates went flying everywhere!

And the three
little monkeys were
jumping and squealing,
And jelly and custard
got stuck
on the ceiling!

So Whiff the beautiful big fat smelly
baby had to go home in disgrace.

For a long time it seemed that Whiff
would never find a friend.
Then one day, Mrs Littlebird knocked on the door.

My baby would
like to play
with your baby.
But tell me, is
your baby
a good baby?

I think he is a good baby.
But Mrs Crocodile says
he is very rough.
And Mrs Monkey says
he is bad-mannered.
They sent him home in disgrace.

And Mrs Littlebird said: "I can see he is beautiful. I can see he is big and fat. But tell me, is he *always* smelly?"

"Always," said Mrs Warthog.

"Never mind," said Mrs Littlebird. "Bring him over."

So Whiff went across the street
to play with Baby Littlebird.
They played happily for hours.
They played trains, planes, doctors and Jungle Monopoly.

But all of a sudden, with a

APP!

SNUP!

The baby bird
ate all the flies up!

And that is how the
beautiful big fat smelly baby
found a friend.